S. Alexander

Mom's Best Friend

Sally Hobart Alexander

Photographs by George Ancona

Macmillan Publishing Company *New York* Maxwell Macmillan Canada *Toronto*

Maxwell Macmillan International *New York* *Oxford* *Singapore* *Sydney*

Many thanks to: Peggy Gibbon, Dolores Holle, Peter Jackson, David Johnson, Paula Pursley, and Doug Roberts, all of The Seeing Eye; and to Ryan Abelman, Kathy Ayres, Shannon Daley, Linda Ellison, Frick International Studies Academy, Sheffy Gordon, Shira Gordon, Joyce Green, Steve Greenberg, Julie Hensley, Marilyn Hollinshead, Warren Hollinshead, Jessica Kennedy, Megan Kennedy, Judy Murphy, Bob Pacheco, and Jennifer Weinberg.

Macmillan Publishing Company is part of the Maxwell Communication Group of Companies. Macmillan Publishing Company, 866 Third Avenue, New York, NY 10022. Maxwell Macmillan Canada, Inc., 1200 Eglinton Avenue East, Suite 200, Don Mills, Ontario M3C 3N1.
First edition. Printed in the United States of America. The text of this book is set in 14 pt. Cushing Book.
10 9 8 7 6 5 4 3 2 1
Library of Congress Cataloging-in-Publication Data
Alexander, Sally Hobart. Mom's best friend / Sally Hobart Alexander ; photographs by George Ancona. — 1st ed.   p.   cm.
Summary: Describes how a blind mother adjusts to getting a new dog guide. ISBN 0-02-700393-0.   1. Guide dogs—Juvenile literature.
[1. Guide dogs.]   I. Ancona, George, ill.   II. Title.
HV1780.A44   1992   362.4'1—dc20   91-43809

To my sister and brother,
Marty Wallen and Bob Hobart,
and to the memory of Marit
                    —S.H.A.

To Lois and Jerome Kuhl
                    —G.A.

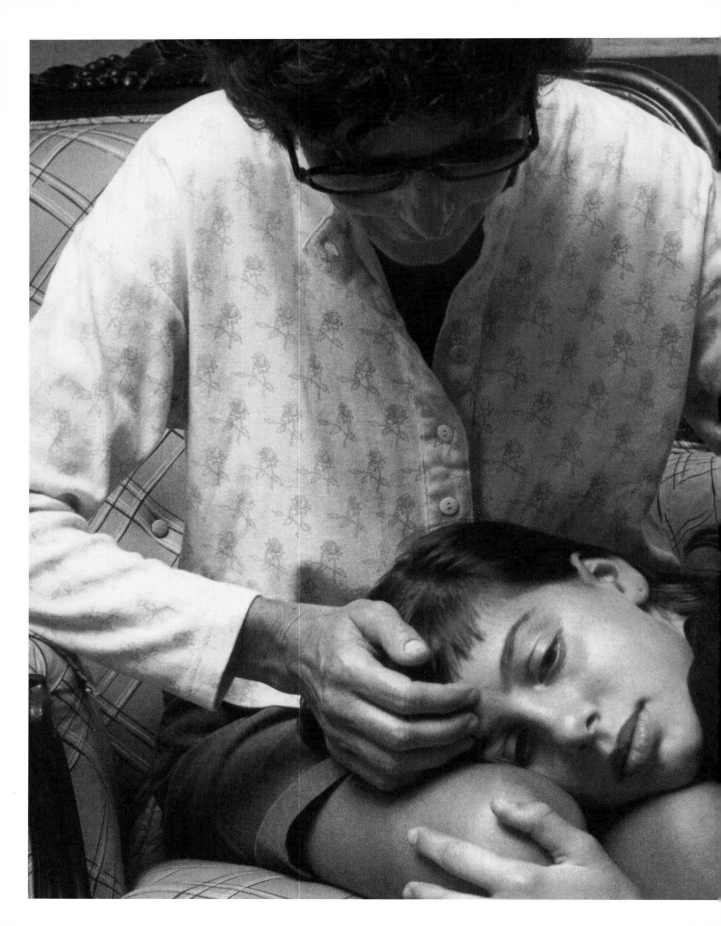

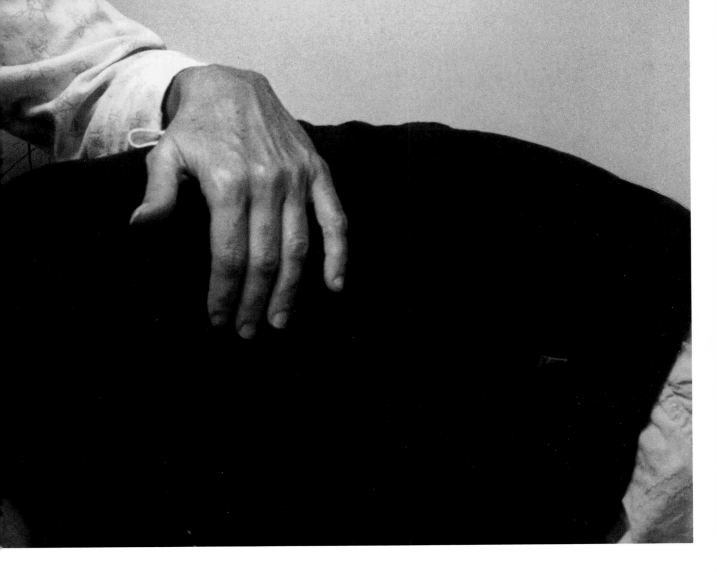

The best thing about having a mom who's blind is getting a special dog like Marit, Mom's dog guide. At least that's what my brother, Joel, and I used to think. Then, four months ago, Marit died. And it became the worst thing.

Marit had been with us since before I was born. Her death left a big hole in our family. I kept thinking I heard her whimpering for a Frisbee game. Any time I left pizza on the counter, I would race back to the rescue. But there was no sneaky dog about to steal it.

For my birthday Joel gave me a rabbit that I named Methuselah. Although it helped to have a soft bunny, I still wanted Marit.

Mom missed her even more. She didn't lose just a sweet, furry pet. She lost her favorite way of traveling, too. She had to use her cane again, and crept along the sidewalk like a snail. Once, when she crossed the street, she missed the opposite curb and kept walking toward the traffic. I had to holler to get her onto the sidewalk.

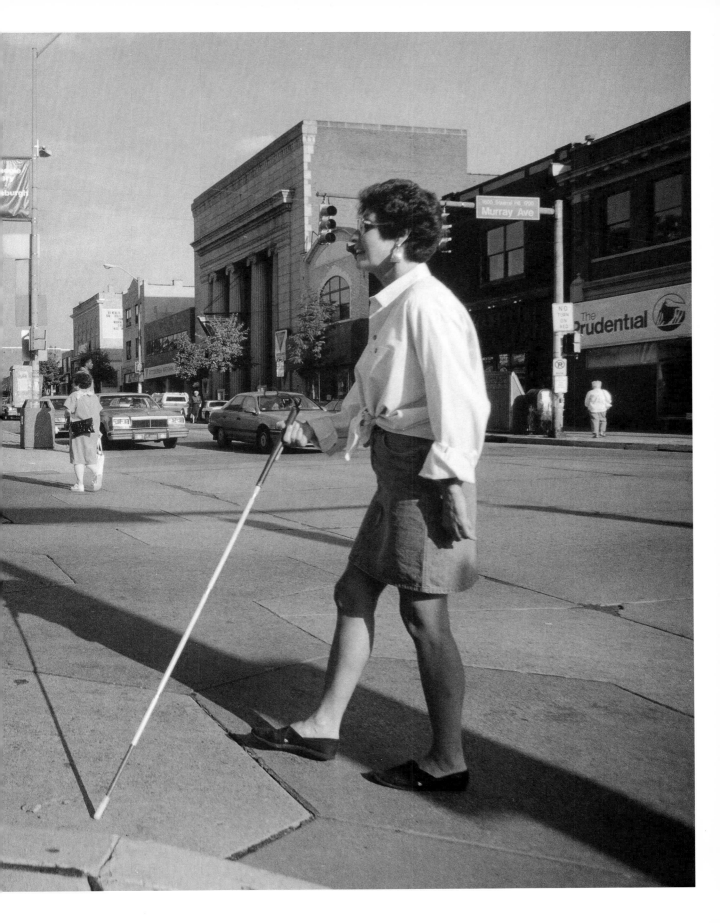

After that, I worried about her running errands by herself. I asked her to "go sighted guide," holding Dad's, Joel's, or my arm. Sometimes she did. But mostly she used the cane. She didn't want to depend on us—or on anybody.

A lot of blind people do fine with a cane. It's like a real long arm to help them feel what's around: walk-ways, hedges, mailboxes.

With a dog guide, blind people use their hearing more than touch. Mom has trained her ears. It's amazing: she can tell when something, like a movie marquee, is above her head, and when she passes a lamppost. She knows from the change in the sound of her footsteps.

In spite of Mom's special hearing, I worried. I was relieved when she decided to go back to The Seeing Eye for a new dog guide.

Before Mom left, I told her I wouldn't be able to love the new dog as much as Marit. Mom hugged me and said, "The night before you were born, I wondered how I could love a second child as much as your brother. Then you came, and like magic, I was just as crazy about you."

The Seeing Eye, in Morristown, New Jersey, was the first dog guide school in the United States. (Now there are nine others.) It trains German shepherds and Labrador and golden retrievers for three months. Then, for about a month, it teaches blind people to use the dogs.

When Mom arrived at The Seeing Eye, she was met by her instructor, Pete Jackson.

I missed Mom as much as I missed Marit, but at least Mom called every night. She also wrote letters and sent pictures.

Mom's first day was a cinch. She'd gone to Seeing Eye twelve years before to get Marit, and still remembered her way around. Usually when she's in a new place, she has to move from room to room with her cane, memorizing the layout.

In the morning Mom walked with Pete Jackson so that he could check her pace. He wanted to choose the dog that would suit her best. Then she was free to play the piano, exercise…and worry. Would she get along with the new dog? Would they work well together?

Sally Alexander
The Seeing Eye
Morristown, N...

The next day she got Ursula. What a strange name! The staff at Seeing Eye's breeding station had named Ursula when she was born. (Ursula's brothers and sisters were also given names starting with *U*.) Dog guides need a name right away so that Seeing Eye can keep track of the four hundred or so pups born each year. At two months of age, the pups go to Seeing Eye puppy-raising families to learn how to live with people. At fifteen months, they are mature enough to return to Seeing Eye for the three-month training program.

Dad said that Ursula means "bear." But in the pictures Mom sent, Ursula looked too pipsqueaky to be called bear. Mom explained that Seeing Eye is now breeding some smaller dogs. They are easier to handle and fit better on buses and in cars.

My friends thought dog guides were little machines that zoomed blind people around. Until Mom went away, even I didn't understand all the things these dogs were taught.

But on Mom's first lesson in Morristown, Ursula seemed to forget her training. She veered on a street crossing and brushed Mom into a bush. Mom had to make her correct herself by backing up and walking around the bush. Then Mom praised her.

After ten practice runs with Pete, Mom and Ursula soloed. Ursula didn't stop at a curb, so Mom had to scold her and snap her leash, calling, "Pfui." Later Ursula crashed Mom into a low-hanging branch. "Ursula will have to start thinking tall," Mom said that night, "or I'll have to carry hedge clippers in my purse."

Even though Ursula had walked in Morristown a lot with Pete, she was nervous when Mom's hand was on the harness. Mom talked and walked differently. And Mom was nervous, too. Ursula moved so much faster than old Marit had, and Mom didn't trust her.

Every day Mom and Ursula made two trips. Every week they mastered new routes. Each route got longer and more complicated, and Mom had less time to learn it. Every night Mom gave Ursula obedience training: "Come. Sit. Down. Rest. Fetch." I thought she should try obedience training on Joel.

While Mom worked hard, Dad, Joel, and I went on with our normal lives—school, homework, soccer, piano, spending time with friends. We divided Mom's chores: Dad did the cooking, Joel, the vacuuming and laundry, and I did the dishes, dusting, weeding. The first two weeks were easy.

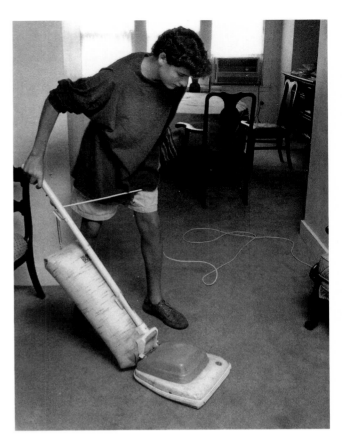

In a phone call Mom said that things were getting easier for her, too. "Remember how tough curb ramps have been for me?" she asked. "They feel like any other slope in the sidewalk, so I can't always tell that I've reached the street. Well, Ursula stopped perfectly at every ramp. And she guided me around, not under, a ladder and right past a huge parking lot without angling into it. But best of all, she actually saved my life. A jackhammer was making so much noise that I couldn't hear whether the light was green or red. When I told Ursula, 'Forward!' she refused to move and kept me from stepping in front of a car. (Of course, Pete would have saved me if Ursula hadn't.)"

Mom barely asked about us. It was all Ursula, Ursula, Ursula! She seemed to be forgetting Marit, too. When a letter came a few days later, I was sure she didn't miss anyone.

Dear Bob, Joel, and Leslie,

Today Ursula and I faced several disasters! She tried hard to ignore a boxer dog who wanted to play. A few minutes later, a great Dane lunged out from nowhere, jumped all over her, and loped off. Ursula's instinct is to chase dogs, but she didn't move a paw after that one. As if the dogs weren't enough trouble, fire engine sirens went off. Ursula just strolled down the sidewalk.

Mostly, life is smooth here. Seeing Eye is a vacation—no cooking, no cleaning, lots of time to talk to new friends, like Dr. Holle, the veterinarian. And since I don't have many blind friends, it's a treat to be with my roommate and the twenty other students. We laugh about the same things, like the great enemy of the blind—trash collection day! Every twenty feet there's a garbage can reeking of pizza, hoagies, old cheese. Usually Ursula snakes me around these smelly obstacles. But sometimes the temptation to her nose wins out, and I have to correct her, all the while holding my own nose.

Some trainees really inspire me, like Julie Hensley, who became blind from diabetes at twenty-two. Even though she's been blind for twelve years, she still teaches horses to do stunts. She judges her location from a radio playing music in the center of the pen, and gallops around as fast as she ever did when she could see.

Bob Pacheco used to race motorcycles and hunt. Then, two years ago, when he was twenty-nine, he developed optic atrophy and became blind two months later. He took up fishing, swimming, even trapping. But something was missing. He couldn't get around quickly enough. After the first trip with his dog guide, he was overjoyed. "Sally!" He grabbed my hand. "I don't feel blind any more."

The dogs are wonderful, and the people here are very special. So are you.

Love,
Mom

Well, life at home wasn't very wonderful or special. Dad ran out of the casseroles Mom had frozen ahead of time, and although his meals were okay, I missed Mom's cooking. Worse, the dishes kept piling up. I never knew Joel ate so much.

Then things got really bad. While Dad was teaching his American literature night class, Joel and I faced a disaster Mom and Ursula couldn't have dreamed of: the toilet bowl overflowed! We wiped the floor with towels. As Joel took the towels down to the washing machine, he found water dripping through the ceiling—all over the dining room table, all over the carpet. He ran for more towels, and I ran for the furniture polish and rug shampoo. When Dad got home, everything looked perfect. But I wrote a braille letter.

Leslie Alexander
5648 Marlborough Rd.
Pittsburgh, PA 15217

Sall
T

Dear Mom,

Come home soon. The house misses you.

Love,

Exhausted in Pittsburgh

Mom wrote back.

Dear Exhausted,

Hang on. We'll be home to "hound" you
Thursday. Be prepared. When you see me,
I will have grown four more feet.

Mom

I couldn't laugh. I was too tired and worried. What if I couldn't love Ursula? Marit
was the best dog ever.

Soon they arrived. Ursula yanked at her leash and sprang up on me. She pawed my shoulders, stomach, and arms just the way Marit used to, nearly knocking me over. She leaped onto Joel, licking him all over. As she bounded up onto me again, I realized Mom was right. Like magic, I was crazy about this shrimpy new dog.

But by the end of the day, I had a new worry. Was *Ursula* going to love *me*? She seemed friendly enough, but keyed up, even lost in our house.

Mom explained that Ursula had already given her heart away three times: first to her mother, then to the Seeing Eye puppy-raising family, and finally to Pete. Mom said we had to be patient.

"Remember how Marit loved you, Leslie? When you were little, she let you stand on her back to see out the window. Ursula will be just as nuts about you. Love is the whole reason this dog guide business works."

So I tried to be patient and watched Mom work hard. First she showed one route in our neighborhood to Ursula and walked it over and over. Then she taught her a new route, repeated that, and reviewed the old one. Every day she took Ursula on two trips, walking two or three miles. She fed her, groomed her, gave her obedience training. Twice a week Mom cleaned Ursula's ears and brushed her teeth.

"I'm as busy as I was when you and Joel were little!" she said.

Mom and Ursula played for forty-five minutes each day. Joel, Dad, and I were only allowed to watch. Ursula needed to form her biggest attachment to Mom.

Mom made Ursula her shadow. When she showered or slept, Ursula was right there.

Still, Ursula didn't eat well—only half the amount she'd been eating at Seeing Eye. And she tested Mom, pulling her into branches, stepping off curbs. Once she tried to take a shortcut home. Another time, because she was nervous, she crossed a new street diagonally.

Crossing streets is tricky. Ursula doesn't know when the light is green. Mom knows. If she hears the cars moving beside her in the direction in which she's walking, the light is green. If they're moving right and left in front of her, it's red.

I worried about Ursula's mistakes, but Mom said they were normal. She kept in touch with her classmates and knew that their dog guides were goofing, too. One kept eating grass, grazing like a cow. Another chased squirrels, pigeons, and cats. Still another always stopped in the middle of the street, ten feet from the curb. Once in a while her friends got lost, just like Mom, and had to ask for help.

Mom said it takes four to six months for the dogs to settle down. But no matter how long she and Ursula are teamed up together, Ursula will need some correcting. For instance, Ursula might act so cute that a passerby will reach out to pet her. Then Mom will have to scold Ursula and ask the person not to pet a dog guide. If people give Ursula attention while she's working, she forgets to do her job.

After a month at home, Ursula emptied her food bowl every time. She knew all the routes, and Mom could zip around as easily as she had with Marit.

"Now it's time to start the loneliness training," Mom said. She left Ursula alone in the house, at first for a short time while she went jogging with Dad. Ursula will never be able to take Mom jogging because she can't guide at high speeds.

Each week Mom increased the amount of time Ursula was alone. I felt sorry for our pooch, but she did well: no barking, no chewing on furniture.

Then Mom said Joel and I could introduce Ursula to
our friends, one at a time. They could pet her when she
was out of harness.

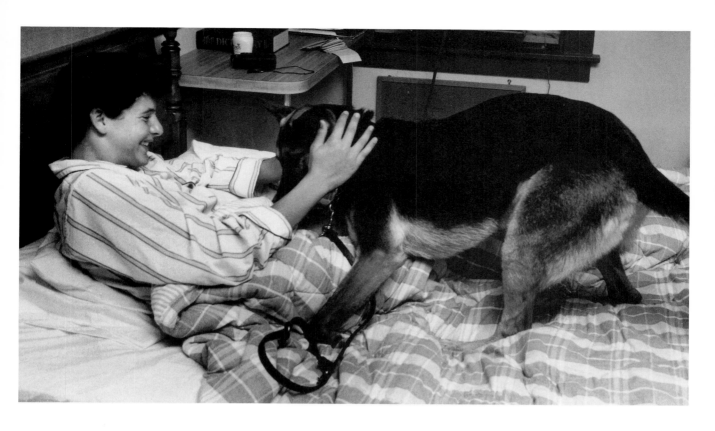

Every morning Ursula woke Joel and me. Every night
she sneaked into my bed for a snooze.

Finally Mom allowed Joel and me to play with Ursula, and I knew: shrimpy little Ursula had fallen for us, and we were even crazier about her.

But we haven't forgotten Marit. Joel says that Ursula is the best dog alive. And I always say she's the best dog in this world.